LILY'S PROMISE

A Victorian Saga

TILLIE WALKER

Live Life Fully Media

PART I

A single tear ran down her cheek as Lily Collins clenched her jaw to keep from weeping uncontrollably. She almost wished she had succumbed to the disease that had killed both her parents, their unmarked graves at her feet. The bluebells she had picked from the nearby woodlands had already started to wilt atop the mound of freshly packed dirt.

The past month had been the worst of Lily's young life. No 17-year old should have to watch as her parents deteriorated each day, their bodies wracked with pain, doubled over with cramps. They would beg her for water but, after a few sips, would expel it again, and afterwards convulse with dry heaves.

Lily looked to the ominous sky. It would be nightfall in a few hours and she still had no idea where she would be sleeping tonight. Her family had been tenant farmers on the land owned by Mr. David Newton. He was known to be a fair and kind squire, but rarely visited the land furthest from the manor house and knew little of the happenings.

In his place, Edmund Smith managed the properties and instilled fear in the tenants. A mean-spirited and miserly man, his wife was barren and some said he beat her for what he perceived as her failure. Mrs. Smith had not been seen outside their cottage in months, and rumour had it that she was crippled and unable to walk, a result of one of the worst beatings. The young women of the village were cautioned to never be caught alone in Edmund Smith's presence, but it was never explained to them exactly why. Lily did not need an explanation, she had no intention of being near the man.

When her parents, Wilbur and Dorrit Collins, first became ill, they tried to hide the fact from both Lily as well as Mr. Smith, fearing they would lose their tenancy if they did not keep up with the plowing and planting at such a critical time of year. But as their symptoms worsened over several weeks, neither could get out of bed. When Edmund Smith visited, he gave them an ultimatum.

"I'll not lose the crops from these acres," he growled. "If the seeds aren't in the ground by the end of the month, you can pack your bags. There are plenty of capable farmers ready to take your place."

As her parents lay in bed with fevers raging, dizzy and nauseous but unable to hold down any food or drink, Lily planted the seeds the way she had seen her father do when she delighted in following along with him in the fields as a young girl. If she could get the planting done on time, it would give her parents time to recover from the illness that kept them in bed.

Truth be told, the Collinses had planned to give up their tenancy themselves after this planting season. Wilbur Collins had been saving every extra penny he could for several years now. It was his dream to move his family to London where he heard there were opportunities for a hard-working man to make a good life for himself and his family. He was saving to buy a handcart and become a costermonger in Covent Garden. He knew fruits and vegetables well, knew how to select the best quality, and was sure his family could thrive. Dorrit and Lily would charm the customers and city life would be an exciting change to the countryside. His daughter was growing up quickly, and London would be a good place for her to find a husband.

EDMUND SMITH WATCHED THE YOUNG COLLINS GIRL FROM HIS vantage point on the hill. She was a comely creature. With her parents dead, he would have to find new tenants for their acreage but there was no reason he could not keep the girl around for his own pleasure.

Smith's wife, Elizabeth, was useless. She had not given him any children and had recently developed a partial paralysis in her legs that resulted in her being bedridden most of the day. Unless he was kind enough to carry her to a chair, where she would sit and read or knit, which he was rarely willing to do. The fact that the paralysis came after one of the particularly brutal beatings he inflicted on her after he had been drinking was lost on him.

With nowhere to go, he was sure Lily Collins would be grateful for his offer of employment. In exchange for her meals and a trundle bed in the corner of his kitchen, he would expect her to cook and clean their home, and tend to his wife's needs, bathing and feeding her, so he wouldn't have to deal with it himself. He would also expect Lily to tend to his needs, although he would not tell her that initially.

With a self-satisfied sneer, he headed down the bluff to make the indelicate offer to the grieving girl.

"MY CONDOLENCES."

Lily started at the voice behind her, having not heard Edmund Smith approach from behind, so lost in her own thoughts was she.

"I'm sorry, I did not mean to startle you," the towering man said as his shadow blocked the warmth of the last of the evening sun, causing Lily to shiver. He rubbed his jowls and Lily was certain she saw gnats jump out of his beard as he did.

She stared at him a moment before speaking. "I will pack my things and clean out our cottage tomorrow, if you would be so kind as to let me sleep the night there." Lily looked up with hopeful eyes. If she could get an early start in the morning, she could manage several miles of walking on her way to London. Perhaps even catch a coach ride for part of the journey.

Smith clasped his hands behind his back and appeared to be considering her request.

"I believe that can be arranged."

"Thank you, Mr. Smith." Lily sighed in relief. "The cottage will be spotless upon my departure and I will vacate the premises at daybreak." She hoped he would forget that her parents had not completed the month's work and, therefore, had technically lived rent free during their illness.

"What are your plans after that?" he asked, licking his lips and then wiping the bit of spittle from the corner of his mouth with a grimy hand.

She started to reply but sensed an inappropriate interest from the glint in his eye and decided not to reveal her intention.

"I ... I am not certain," she said. "I shall find employment."

Mr. Smith nodded, as if this revelation was the first he considered her future. "Of course, of course." He stepped back, started to turn and leave, then stopped as if he had a sudden burst of inspiration.

"Miss Collins, perhaps I can be of some assistance," he began, pausing to see if he had her interest. "It is quite a private matter, but my wife has not been well of late, and is fairly immobile. Nothing I cannot deal with myself, naturally, but seeing as you are in need of employment, I would be prepared to offer you an arrangement whereby you care for her well-being in exchange for room and board in our home."

The offer surprised Lily, but rather than a feeling of gratitude, the hair on the back of her neck prickled, causing a feeling of foreboding like none she had experienced previously. The sooner she left this place, the better.

"That is very kind of you, Mr. Smith," she began. "I am truly sorry to hear of your wife's affliction. I regret I am unable to accept your generous offer, however. I plan to fulfill the wishes of my parents." She paused, then added, "My father has a brother who they wished for me to join." She hoped Smith would accept her excuse and not probe for details about the non-existent uncle.

Mr. Smith took a deep breath as a red hue rose in his cheeks and the pupils of his eyes turned to small pricks. Lily feared she had offended the man, but he responded with an even, albeit sinister, voice.

"Very well, Miss Collins. As you wish."

He turned and strode purposefully away in the direction from which he had approached her.

Lily let out a breath, unaware she had been holding it. She took one last look at her parents' grave and walked slowly back to the cottage they had shared for as long as she could remember.

◌⁕◌

ONCE SHE HAD SCRUBBED THE FLOORS AND DUSTED THE shelves, Lily packed her few essential belongings into a small bag that she felt would be light enough to be manageable on her journey to London. Her stomach grumbled, reminding her that she had not eaten anything all day, so she broke off a chunk of bread and cut herself a generous chunk of cheese. She would save the rest for her journey, not knowing how long it would take or where she would find food and shelter along the way.

She sat at the small table where she had shared meals with her parents, eating the meagre meal as she counted out the savings her father kept hidden in a tin. She hoped it would be enough to last until she reached London and found employment.

A rap on the wooden door startled her out of her musings and she quickly scooped the coins back into the tin, hiding it behind a pitcher on a shelf, before timidly approaching the door.

"Who is there please?" She asked timidly.

"It's Mr. Smith. I'm afraid I forgot to discuss some unfinished business with you earlier."

L ily hesitated, then through the heavy door asked, "What is it?"

"Open the door, Miss Collins. It will only take a moment but is a rather delicate matter concerning your parents."

Instinct told her not to open the door, but she did not know how to avoid it. The nearest cottage of the next tenant's family was at least a mile away, and she could not think of a plausible reason to refuse to open the door.

She nervously unlatched the hook that locked the door in place and opened it.

Mr. Smith barged into the small cottage, filling it with his stature so that it felt claustrophobic and crowded at once.

"I'm sorry to have to tell you this in your time of mourning, but I was checking my ledger, and the rent on this cottage has not been paid this month. Between that, and the lack of work completed, there is a balance due before you vacate the estate."

Tears welled in Lily's eyes and she pinched herself under her wrap to stop herself from blubbering.

"I finished the planting myself this month, Mr. Smith. Even

though my parents were ill." She looked at him with pleading eyes.

"Miss Collins, even if I were to consider your efforts to be equal to what was required, there is still the matter of the rent. That alone is six shillings owed."

She swallowed hard. Six shillings was the better part of the savings she had for her journey to London.

Smith continued. "Now if you would like to reconsider my offer of employment, your first two months would serve to repay your parents' debts. After that, you are free to go."

He reached out and put his hand on her arm, rubbing it slowly, before slipping his hand higher. His calloused thumb rubbed her cheek and he grinned, panting with anticipation. She tried to pull away but he hooked his meaty hand behind her neck, caressing her bare skin, and squeezed her delicate throat. He yanked her abruptly forward, but she was nimble and managed to twist away and jump back.

"I can pay the rent!" she said, quickly retreating to a distance that was out of his reach.

Incensed by her obvious disgust of his advances, Smith's face twisted in anger. With one stride forward, he grabbed the front of her smock and pulled her toward him, tearing it in the process. He wrapped his other arm around her waist and dragged her closer, his body pressed against hers.

Lily screamed but he muffled the sound by crushing his mouth over her own, thrusting his thick tongue inside so deeply she nearly gagged as the taste of tobacco and alcohol overwhelmed her.

With one swift move, he tore the dress from her shivering frame and threw her onto the bed, holding her down with one beefy forearm while untethering his belt with his other hand.

Struggling proved to be hopeless and only caused her more pain. The last thing she remembered, Lily was squeezing her eyes shut and praying that the ordeal would be over quickly.

ONCE EDMUND SMITH HAD SATISFIED HIMSELF AND THE GIRL'S whimpers became an annoyance to him, he heaved his body off the bed and began to redress. As he sauntered towards the door, he remembered something and stopped.

"You said you could pay. Where is it?"

Lily groaned and curled herself into the foetal position, burying her head and refusing to look up at her assailant.

"Never mind. I'll find it myself. This place is small enough it shouldn't take long to search."

Edmund Smith swept the room methodically, upending pots and pans and plates, cursing as each upturned piece revealed nothing. He moved toward the shelf and reached up to grab the pitcher to look inside. When he did, he found the tin that Lily had carefully replaced hidden behind the pitcher.

A satisfied grin revealed a mouth of yellowing teeth as he retrieved the tin and opened it to reveal the coins.

"No!" Lily had dared to lift her head, watching him find the paltry savings that represented years of toil for her family. The insignificant sum would be a pittance for someone like him but could be the difference between survival and despair for Lily. "It's all I have!"

"And now it's mine," he said, a snide grin on his face. "Would you rather be sent to debtor's prison for the unpaid bills of your father? Be gone by daybreak or I may decide you have not settled your debts after all."

IT WAS STILL DARK OUTSIDE WHEN LILY CLOSED THE COTTAGE door behind her for the last time. She pulled the wool shawl that had belonged to her mother tighter around her shoulders against the chill in the air. The warm, inviting home that she shared with her parents for most of her life would never hold the same memories after the degradation she had suffered at the hands of Edmund Smith.

Lily did not dare wait until daybreak to be on her way lest the vile man return. She carried what was left of the bread and cheese with her but would wait until she had walked a couple of hours, and put plenty of distance between her and the estate, before stopping to eat.

She was sore from the attack and walking was painful but she had managed to stop the bleeding she had suffered from the brutal assault. She trudged gingerly along the overgrown country path in the general direction of London.

She had no idea what she might find once she arrived, if indeed she managed to make it that far. Would she find work? A safe place to live? Her father had often spoken of the riches in London and the opportunities there. His eyes would light up every time they discussed it together at the small dining table.

After a couple of hours, she stopped by the side of the road and perched on a boulder. The sun had risen and warmed the air, so she removed the shawl and folded it carefully, placing it in her valise with her most cherished personal items that she had selected to bring along. She ate just enough bread to give her the energy to continue on her way, determined to keep moving forward and put the past behind her.

●

THE WEATHER CHANGED AGAIN IN THE LATE AFTERNOON AND Lily withdrew her mother's cloak once more and wrapped it around her as protection from the strong winds. She knew she would soon need to find shelter for the night and wished she had stopped a half-mile back when she passed a cottage that had a storage barn far enough away from the road that she could likely go undetected for the night.

The wind was howling so fiercely that she did not hear the large steed galloping down upon her. By the time she had seen the imposing horse and rider, it was too late to hide in the brush and she froze in terror.

"Whoa." The rider reigned in his stallion and held the skittish animal as best he could in order to take in the disheveled girl. "Miss, is everything all right? Do you need assistance?"

"I'm fine, thank you." Lily lowered her head and began to walk.

"It's getting dark, Miss. And a storm is brewing."

Lily's heart was pounding so hard she thought she could hear it. *Please, God, no. Do not let me suffer yet another attack.* She continued to walk and refused to look at the stranger.

The rider dismounted, took his horse by the reigns and started to walk beside Lily.

"Please leave me be," she said.

"I don't mean to frighten you, Miss, but you are miles from town and the weather is turning. Do you live nearby? I would be happy to see you safely where you are going."

Lily spun around to confront the man, but when she did, there was something so kind in his eyes that her instinct told her she was in no danger. She hoped she was right because she was dead on her feet and could barely take another step.

"I'm on my way to London," she said, aware of how vulnerable she was and that she was taking a tremendous risk by admitting that to the man.

"Well, now, you would still have another long day or two ahead of you to reach London on foot. You are about an hour or more away from the nearest inn for the night. But if you'll allow me, I'd be happy to take you to London tonight. That's where I'm headed." He waited while she considered his offer. When she didn't speak for nearly a full minute he said, "We need to get on the road if we're going to make it tonight. Up to you whether you say yes or not, but the offer is there."

"I don't have any money to pay you for your trouble," she said.

He smiled. "No trouble at all. And I'm sure Prince here won't mind. You don't look like you weigh more than eight stone. Here, let me give you a boost up and we'll be in London in no time."

His name was George Cole and he owned a public house in the City. He regaled Lily with stories of life in the city that both amused and frightened her. George cautioned her not to be lured into a house of ill repute, a fate that caught many young ladies new to the City unaware. Unfortunately, mention of this brought the memory of her attack flooding back to her, something she was trying hard to forget.

Lily told George about her father's dream of selling fruits and vegetables in Covent Garden and that she might seek employment with a costermonger there, but he suggested she might wish to seek a position in domestic service which would provide her not only with a job, but also a place to live and meals. Several of his regular patrons held positions in nearby homes from among the new middle class ranks, the bankers and merchants who had recently risen in social standing. He told her he would ask around to see if anyone was seeking household help.

They arrived in Holborn on the outskirts of the City of London in the wee hours of the morning. George assisted Lily from the stallion before dismounting and tying the horse to a post in the alley behind the public house.

The wooden door opened and a woman holding a lantern greeted them with a wide grin.

"I thought I heard something back here. Just checking to see if it was a someone up to no good."

"Ada, this is Miss Collins," George said to the woman who was standing before them in her night dress. "Miss Collins has come to London all the way from Hertfordshire to make her fortune in the City."

The woman stuck her hand out and shook Lily's with a vice-like grip. "Ada Cole, dear. Welcome to London."

"Lily Collins." Lily rubbed her hand after Ada released it to get the circulation back in her fingers.

"I thought Miss Collins could sleep in the pantry tonight. I'll ask around tomorrow and see if any of the locals know of a domestic position she might be considered for."

Lily was stunned by the continued kindness of the man whom she'd come to know over the course of their journey to London, not to mention the graciousness of Ada Cole who seemed just as welcoming. "You've already been so kind to bring me to London, Mr. Cole. I could not impose further."

Ada Cole spoke up before George had a chance to reply. "Nonsense, dear. Offering our pantry floor is no imposition at all. Nor any luxury." She cackled at her own joke before continuing. "The City wakes up in a few short hours so you better come in and get some sleep."

With that, she turned around and ascended the staircase, leaving George to sort out a corner in the pantry with a few blankets for Lily to rest.

❦

THE SIGHTS AND SOUNDS OF LONDON WERE A WONDER TO behold. More than once, Lily was nearly trampled by a carriage when she failed to jump out of the way. The smells of the city were not quite the same as Hertfordshire either, and she was glad she carried a handkerchief with her to hold over her nose and mouth as she navigated the teeming streets.

George and Ada Cole had offered her refuge until she found a domestic servant position and she had insisted on carrying her weight by helping with the washing up of tankards, glasses and plates from the pub. Although she stayed out of sight, she was fascinated by the cacophony of voices shouting throughout the evening, becoming louder as the night wore on.

On her fourth day in London, George gave her the good news that he had found a position for her.

"It's only a scullery maid, but if you do well, you might be able to progress to a kitchen maid or laundry maid in due course."

Lily arrived at the terraced house on John Street in Bloomsbury at 7:50 AM, ten minutes early for her appointment with Mrs. Evans, the housekeeper of the Williams residence. John Williams was a banker on Threadneedle Street and expected an impeccably run household to which Mrs. Evans was happy to comply.

"You are older than the usual scullery maid," she said to Lily. "And with no experience."

"I've been helping my parents manage a farm and household since I could walk. I'm reliable and conscientious and hard working." Lily widened her eyes and looked at Mrs. Evans in earnest. When the older woman did not reply immediately, Lily added, "If you'll just give me a chance, I won't let you down."

"Very well. You can start immediately. Laura will explain your duties and give you a uniform to wear. You'll sleep in the room behind the kitchen. You will be provided with your meals and a salary of one shilling per week. You'll be called Mary, as is the custom of a scullery maid."

Mrs. Evans abruptly exited the room before Lily had even had a chance to thank her for giving her a chance.

HER EXCITEMENT AT HAVING SECURED EMPLOYMENT AS WELL AS a place to live was short-lived as she listened with trepidation to Laura explain what was expected of her.

"The footman will knock you up at 5 o'clock before he goes round to light the fires in all the rooms on the main floor. Except the kitchen fire. That's your job. You'll set the water over to boil. Then you'll sweep the front steps and wash the kitchen floor before Cook arrives. When the oven fire is hot, you will bake the breakfast rolls. Those you should mix and prepare the prior night, before you go to bed. Otherwise, you'll have to get up at 4:30 to get it done."

Laura went on to tell Lily how she'd be helping with the laundry and scrubbing. She would be picking, trimming, washing, and cutting the vegetables. Lily would be required to fetch and pump water, to wash all the pots and pans that were used in meal preparation each day, polish the silver — which Mrs. Evans would count every evening to ensure nothing was missing — and keep all the kitchen utensils clean and ready for use throughout the day.

Laura then showed Lily where she would sleep. Mrs. Evans had mentioned a room behind the kitchen but it was little more than a cupboard. A thin mattress that was barely longer than Lily's petite 5'3" height lay on the floor and there was hardly space left for her small valise in the remaining space beside the bed. The room was not heated but Laura assured Lily that it was usually warm enough from the kitchen heat that spilled over.

"It's the summertime that's the worst," Laura said. "Gets so hot in here you can hardly breathe."

Lily looked around and realised the space did not have a window.

"Here are two uniforms for you. It's your responsibility to make sure they are clean and pressed. And I'll warn you now that you best be wearing a clean one each and every morning." Laura handed her two stiff cotton black dresses and crisp white aprons. "You can change now, Mary, and meet me back in the kitchen."

"It's Lily, actually."

"Scullery maid is always Mary. The uniform. Quickly."

Lily set her valise in the corner and removed her best dress that she had worn to apply for the job. She slipped into the black dress and buttoned the multiple buttons. It was a bit loose, but she added the apron and wrapped the belt around her waist, then back to the front where she cinched it.

The remainder of the day was a blur as she followed Laura around the kitchen, learning what was expected of her. She cut her finger chopping vegetables, burned her hand when she reached for the cast iron skillet without benefit of a pot holder, and ripped her apron when she got it stuck in the oven door. It was a breakneck pace and more strenuous work than the farm had been, even when Lily did the planting on her own while her parents were sick.

When the other household servants sat down to eat the evening meal together, Lily learned that she was not to join them. The scullery made was required to stay in the kitchen and keep an eye on the food that was still being served to the Williams family. Only after serving was finished and she had washed all the dishes, scrubbed all the pots and pans, and mopped the floor, was Lily permitted to eat from among the leftovers that the other servants had not consumed for their own meal.

By 10 o'clock, she was more tired than hungry, but forced herself to eat some soup with a few chunks of meat, and a generous amount of potatoes and onions. She collapsed on the mattress in her cupboard and fell asleep without even changing out of her uniform.

4

The days turned to weeks and the weeks to months. Lily could not remember how long she had been serving at the Williams residence nor how many consecutive days she had worked without a day off.

The work was excruciatingly hard, physically but also mentally, trying to remember the order of the tasks to be completed lest Cook be angry if something wasn't just right. At 5 o'clock, the footman, Gerald, would knock on her door and she would rise, bleary eyed and astonished that it was morning already. She often felt as if she had just fallen asleep when it was time to start another day.

Gerald was not much older than her and had taken a liking to her. Seeing she was having a difficult time coping with the intensity of the work, Gerald would usually light the kitchen fire for Lily before moving onto the sitting rooms where he was required to open the shutters, deliver the coal that would be needed throughout the day and light fires.

Lily set the water over to boil on the kitchen stove and went about her mind-numbing chores. Each day required cleaning, peeling and chopping vegetables. Depending on the meals to be served, she might scrub the scales off fish or pluck the feathers from a hen. It was her sole responsibility to scour all the pots and pans, mop the floors at least twice per day, and clear all the garbage and debris from the kitchen counters and floor.

If Mrs. Evans sensed that she had any spare time whatsoever, which was impossible to believe could happen, but often did, Lily would be commissioned to assist the laundry maid, particularly on days when the household linens had to be changed.

Lily thought that with practice, the work would become easier, but it was not to be. In fact, she was becoming more tired by the day and had taken to feeling ill, particularly on the days when kippers were prepared for the morning breakfast. On one occasion, she was so overcome with the smell that she had to race outdoors to vomit. Unfortunately, that was the day that Mrs. Evans chose to visit Cook and witnessed Lily clutching her stomach, her face white as a ghost.

The housekeeper scowled, raised her eyebrows and looked at Cook, who in turn shook her head with a weary sigh.

On this particular day, Lily had the afternoon off, her first in nearly three months, and she was feeling slightly better than she had since her first day on the job. She decided to pay a visit to Ada Cole to let her and George know that she had indeed been hired for the job that George had recommend her for, and that she was still in London and doing well. Or at least that she was living and working in London.

She remembered the public house in Holborn was only about fifteen minutes walk from the Williams residence, yet when she set out on the journey, it all seemed so foreign and new to her, she'd been cooped up in the scullery of the terraced house for so long. She took extra time to stop in the green square on the way and breathe in the damp air.

ADA OPENED THE DOOR IN THE ALLEY BEHIND THE PUBLIC house and could not believe her eyes. She grabbed the hands of the younger woman and pulled her into the hallway, embracing her in a bear hug.

"We wondered what's become of you, my dear," she said as she practically squeezed the breath out of Lily.

Ada was stunned at Lily's appearance. Her eyes were sunken and she appeared to have aged ten years. Oddly, her dress appeared too small for her, the fabric strained across her belly.

"I wanted you to know that I secured the job that Mr. Cole recommended me for. I came to thank him. And you. For being so kind to me."

"It was nothing," Ada said. "Come upstairs and let me make you a nice cup of tea. George is in the pub. I'll let 'im know you're here."

In twenty minutes, Lily was settled at Ada's kitchen table, her hands clutching a cup of tea, the warmth comforting against her chapped hands. She told Ada a bit about her work, trying to sound positive, not wanting to sound ungrateful despite the arduous physical labor and punishing schedule. It did not take long before Ada recognised the challenge that Lily was facing.

"Is there not something more you want to tell me, dear?" she asked.

Lily looked puzzled. "It's quite hard work, but I'm hoping to advance to housemaid soon. Then I will be allowed to take my meals with the other servants and my work days won't be quite so long." She looked expectantly at Ada, hoping her response was what she anticipated.

Ada lowered her voice and gently said, "I was referring to the baby. How far along are you?"

Lily's eye widened in horror. "Baby! Whatever are you talking about?"

When Ada reached over and took the tea cup from her hands and set it down on the table before grasping Lily's hands in her own, Lily knew. She had thought it was the brutal work and never-ending fatigue that caused the changes in her body, the reason she had not experienced the monthly bleeding. She attributed the perpetual stench of the City and smells of food in the stifling kitchen, the lack of air in her small sleep space, as the cause for her vomiting. But why would her clothes be getting tighter around her waist despite that she barely had enough to eat to keep her on her feet all day.

A tear ran down her cheek as the awareness grew. She was carrying Edmund Smith's child.

Ada sensed the young girl's distress. "You did not know." It was a statement, not a question. "What about the father? Have you any idea when you might have conceived?"

Lily was openly weeping now. "It happened two days before I arrived in London. I must go now." She stood up and ran to the staircase. She was feeling sick and needed air.

"What's this I hear about a visitor!" George Cole nearly crashed into Lily as he bounded into the kitchen. "Ada, I'll have a cup of that tea. Let me take a look at our Miss Collins, a grown up London working woman now."

"Hel...lo, Mr. Cole." Lily swallowed hard. "I'm sorry. I must be getting back now. I just wanted to thank you. For recommending me for the job." She tried to slip past him but George Cole caught her arm and looked into her sorrowful eyes.

"We'll hear none of you rushing off just minutes after you've arrived. You look tired, girl. I know the job of scullery maid is the toughest in the house, but with your will and determination, I can see you rising to a lady's maid or housekeeper one day. Now sit back down and Ada will make us all some supper."

The continued kindness of this couple was enough to over-whelm Lily and she sat back down at the table while Ada ladled hot stew into bowls for the three of them. Lily's eyes met George's and all she saw was love and kindness. Ada was a lucky woman.

After they had eaten and were ready to say their goodbyes, the Coles made Lily promise that she would visit every month on her afternoon off, which Lily was eager to accept. She wrapped her shawl around her and hugged each of them before stepping outside into the chilly air to return to the stifling room behind the kitchen that was now her home.

She had a lot to think about and wondered how she would cope with a baby on the way.

❧

ONCE LILY DEPARTED, ADA CLEARED THE DISHES FROM THE table while George lit a cigarette. She was pensive and uncertain whether she should broach the subject with him. When she had watched him earlier, there was something in the way he looked at the girl that gave her pause. He had feelings for her, of that she was sure. But did it go beyond that?

"The girl is with child," she said.

George's head jolted up to stare at Ada and he sat motionless for a few moments. The lit match he held in his hand burned close to his fingers until he felt the warmth and blew it out.

"She told you that?" he asked.

"I told her. I could see it right away and when I asked, at first she tried to deny it, but after thinking about it, accepted it was the truth."

"Poor thing." George withdrew another match and lit his cigarette. "Life is not easy for an unwed mother."

"She said it happened about the same time she came to London." Ada was apprehensive about what she was about to suggest. "About the time you met her and brought her here." She paused to give him time to consider what she was implying.

"Now just a minute there, Ada," he sprang to his feet. "What are you suggesting?"

"I see the way you look at her, George."

"I did not touch that girl." His distress at her accusation was obvious. "I discovered her just as I told you. On the road to London, exhausted and scared."

He pulled out his chair and sat back down. After a stiff gaze in Ada's direction to put the shameful thought out of her mind, he became pensive. "Now that I think back, though, I was certain there was more to her fear than just her parents' death. When I first stopped to see if she needed help, she went white as a ghost and looked at me as if I was going to attack her."

"I believe you," Ada said. "We'll keep an eye on her as best we can over the coming months. That girl is going to need a lot of support, and some good friends."

George nodded, glad that Ada had a kind heart despite the adversity she had dealt with in her own life.

5

Each month, Lily counted the days until her afternoon off when she could visit Ada and George Cole. Mr. Cole would always leave the pub in the capable hands of his bartender for a few hours and join Lily and Ada for a hearty meal that included meat, potatoes, vegetables and bread. Sometimes Ada would add a chunk of cheese and some butter. It was the Coles' most elaborate meal of the month and they often scrimped in the week leading up to Lily's visit because they knew how much she needed the sustenance. Occasionally, Lily would spend a penny of her wages on three eggs which she would take to her friends, and Ada would boil them for a special treat.

Lily became more relaxed in their company and shared stories of her parents and their life as tenant farmers. Thinking back, it was actually a fine life, with lots of fresh air and nutritious food that they cultivated themselves.

Ada and George had both been born in London and always lived near the city centre. The day that Lily had met George was one of his rare journeys to the outskirts of the city to purchase supplies for the pub at a far lower price than he could get if he bought from one of the local vendors.

Lily was envious their obvious devotion to one another. She hoped that one day she might find a kind man like George to care about her. Sometimes she would catch George staring at her and thought he must be pitying her situation. If she caught his eye, he would turn away and appear embarrassed that he had been watching her.

Lily enjoyed hearing tales of the City and looked forward to the day she would have more time and energy to explore and experience it for herself. For now, she was preoccupied with the baby growing in her belly and thoughts of how she would survive as her pregnancy became more visible. Not to mention, how long she would be able to carry out her duties.

Her belly seemed to grow bigger each day and, thus far, she managed to hide it under the uniform with its roomy apron. However, what was once a too-large dress for her petite frame was now creating concern because she could no longer clasp all of the buttons. She noticed Laura glancing sideways at her several times as they worked side-by-side in the kitchen earlier in the week.

Then the day she feared became a reality.

"Mary. A word." Mrs. Evans curtly moved from the kitchen towards the office that she occupied to take care of the accounts and invoices and count out the weekly wages for each of the staff under her control. She sat down behind the desk but did not invite Lily to take a chair, leaving her standing in front of the desk.

"Yes, ma'am," she said.

"It has been brought to my attention that you are infirm and unable to fulfil the obligations to which you were employed. Is that correct?"

Lily was shocked. She had not missed a step in her work, had not overslept. She still arose long before all the other household staff and went to bed well after everyone else.

"No, ma'am." Her voice quivered as she answered the woman

who held the power to change her circumstances in an instant. "I am fulfilling all of my duties as assigned."

"Do you deny you are with child?"

Lily bowed her head. "No, ma'am."

"Just when were you planning to tell me that I would soon need to find another scullery maid to replace you? Did you not think of the good of this household? Not to mention the shame you bring to the honourable family who employs you, and the other staff. Am I to understand that there is no father to support you and the child?"

Lily started to weep uncontrollably. She had planned to be strong and to continue to work as hard as always until the baby was born. She realised that she had not really thought any of it properly through.

"Stop your crying. I cannot handle such a sign of weakness in my staff." Mrs. Evans stood up, a signal that Lily was dismissed from her presence. "Get back to work and I shall summon you once I've decided what to do with you."

※

ADA COLE WAS THOUGHTFUL AFTER LILY'S MOST RECENT VISIT. Whatever would the girl do once her employer discovered she was pregnant without benefit of marriage. She was certain it would be soon based on how her belly was growing.

"George, I have an idea and I want you to hear me out," she said one evening after they had finished their tea.

She sat across the table from him and waited until he looked directly into her eyes, giving him her full attention. He pushed his plate away and sat up straight in the hard chair.

"What is it, Ada?"

"I would like to adopt Lily's baby."

He hesitated before replying. He did not want to upset her but was ambivalent about her plan. Ada was childless herself and he thought she had finally learned to accept that she would never have one of her own.

"Do you think that's a good idea?" He asked. "I thought you had accepted the fact that you would never have children."

"Accepting it and liking it are two different things," she said. "This feels like a gift from God. Like it was meant to be." Her voice rose with animation. "Why else would you have stumbled across a stranger on your travels? A young, pregnant girl who has no one else. Who needs our help?" She was imploring him now.

"I don't know, Ada," he said. "Raising a baby takes a lot of energy. You aren't a young woman any more. And Lily has not even indicated that she wishes to give her baby up for adoption."

"What choice does she have?" Ada asked. "If she wishes, she can see the baby any time."

"And what if she wants the child back? Once she becomes more stable and can provide a home?"

Ada sighed. "Promise me that we can at least talk to her about it? On her next visit." She started at him in silence for a long time. "Please."

⚜

Two weeks after Lily admitted her pregnancy to Mrs. Evans, she was back in the woman's office. This time, Mrs. Evans instructed her to sit down in the hard-backed chair that was positioned directly across from the desk. The housekeeper wheeled forward on her squeaky office chair and folded her hands on the desk in front of her.

Lily tried to fold her own hands in her lap but her bulging belly was making it difficult. She was now acutely aware that her work was suffering from her expanding girth and increasing fatigue. She feared she would be dismissed and wondered if she would have the courage to go to Ada and George Cole for help. She wasn't due to visit them again for another couple of weeks.

"Mary," Mrs. Evans began. "I've been making some inquiries into options that might be available to you in your ... shall we say ... situation. I assume you do not currently have a plan for how you will live and manage once the child is born?"

Lily was ashamed to admit that she was no closer to a solution than the day she had discovered she was pregnant. "No, ma'am, I do not. But I know I can still do my work. I hoped I could stay on here." She lowered her head, embarrassed to meet Mrs. Evans' eyes, lest she see the disdain in them. Just speaking the words, she realised how presumptuous and foolish the idea was that she could have a baby and remain employed and living in this home.

Her head snapped up, however, when she heard the unexpected words.

"I believe we can allow you to retain your position," the housekeeper said. "Under certain conditions. If that is what you wish."

Lily sat taller in her chair, her hand on her belly as she felt the kick from within, as if her baby had heard the news and was acknowledging that everything was going to be all right. "Yes, it is! Thank you, Missus."

Mrs. Evans held up her hand. "Of course, you cannot remain here with a baby. Luckily, I have been able to find a suitable home for the child. Once it is born."

Lily's face sunk and turned pale. "What do you mean?"

Mrs. Evans explained to Lily that she had found a nurse who placed the babies of unwed mothers, with no other options to care for the children themselves, into the homes of childless married couples who would care for the newborn. In some cases, it was intended only until the mother was able to provide a home for the child, usually if she managed to find a husband. In other cases, the foster parents would adopt the child and raise it as their own.

In Lily's case, the nurse had found a married couple living in the country who were willing to care for Lily's baby, for a fee.

"You will pay 10 pounds in advance and then half of your salary will be withheld and given to the couple to pay for the ongoing costs of raising the child," Mrs. Evans explained.

"I don't have 10 pounds," Lily said, panic rising in her voice. If she could not pay and could not find another job, she might be sent to Debtor's prison. She knew that she could not go to a workhouse as she would now be labeled an immoral woman.

Mrs. Evans appeared to be thoughtful, opened her desk drawer and withdrew a journal. She made a couple of calculations with a pencil and then looked up at the girl.

"Very well. We will have to advance the fee for you from your future salary and keep the other half that does not go for your child's care until the debt is paid off." She snapped the journal closed and replaced it in the desk drawer, turning a key and slipping the key into the pocket of her apron.

As she made the calculations in her own head, Lily wondered if she would ever be able to save enough money to provide a home of her own for her baby. But what choice did she have? At least her baby would be cared for, be fed, and raised in the country which she thought was a healthier environment than London. And for the time being, she had a place to sleep, food and a job for herself.

Mrs. Evans prodded her for a decision, clearly ready to finish the distasteful conversation and get back to her other duties. "What other option do you have, Mary?" she asked.

❧

LILY WAS DEVASTATED FOR THE REMAINDER OF THE DAY AFTER signing the piece of paper presented to her by Mrs. Evans, effectively handing over her newborn to be raised elsewhere as soon as he or she entered the world. As if sensing what had happened, her baby's kicks were more pronounced than ever for the rest of the day. Lily held her hand on her belly and reassured the unborn child.

"I promise I will come and visit you every chance I get. And as soon as it's possible, I will bring you home with me," she whispered. "Just hang on, and I promise I'll make it up to you."

🌼

ADA WAS PREPARING AN EXTRA SPECIAL TREAT FOR THEIR supper today. It had been nearly a month since they had last seen Lily and it would be the day that Ada would suggest that Lily allow her to adopt her baby.

Ada was nervous. She hoped that Lily would not find the proposition offensive, but she would promise to give the child the best of care in a loving environment. And Lily could visit any time and be part of the baby's life. Ada had a feeling that George had a soft spot for the girl and would be happy to keep her in their life.

The table was set and the meaty stew was simmering. Ada had made it chunkier than usual, with meat, carrots, onions and potatoes. She also baked a fresh loaf of bread and scavenged a ripe chunk of cheddar from the pub.

Lily usually arrived just after one o'clock in the afternoon. She and Ada would have a cup of tea until George joined them, sometime before two o'clock. As she refolded the linens and re-stirred the soup for the umpteenth time, Ada fretted because Lily was late.

At a quarter to two, George entered the warm kitchen and inhaled deeply. "Smells heavenly, Ada. You've outdone yourself."

"Lily hasn't arrived yet," she said, her brow furrowed.

"She might be moving more slowly these days," George said. "Last time we saw her, she seemed dragged down by the extra weight. Let's have some tea while we wait."

Two o'clock quickly became two-thirty and then three

o'clock. By four o'clock, it was dusk and George and Ada had to accept that Lily was not coming for her usual visit today.

"Do you think she might be having the baby?" George asked.

"If she is, it's several weeks early," Ada replied. "Which is never a good thing."

"You think I should go 'round and inquire?"

After some deliberation, George and Ada decided that George would wait until the following day when he would check with the housekeeper at Lily's employer to be sure she was all right. He certainly hoped nothing was wrong. He had grown fond of her and felt a protectiveness for her that was difficult to let go.

6

Lily was exhausted and could not comprehend how she would walk to the Coles' home today for her monthly visit. Mrs. Evans had made it clear to her that she would be expected to perform her full duties until the baby was born, which meant she was getting up earlier and staying up later than usual to compensate for her sluggishness. Everything took longer to accomplish.

It was the day she was normally entitled to half a day off, meaning it was her day to visit George and Ada, but she was running late in order to finish her tasks.

Just as she was ready to grab her coat from the hook and make the fifteen minute walk to Holborn, she doubled over in pain and felt a gush of liquid at her feet. She screamed.

Laura came running from the kitchen to find Lily crouched on the floor, crying and holding her belly. The girl who had become her friend in the months since she'd been working at the Williams residence quickly sprang into action.

"Let's get you into bed and I'll run for Mrs. Evans. She'll call the midwife."

Five excruciating hours later and Lily heard the blood-curdling scream of her newborn infant, seconds after he had been removed from her womb.

"It's a boy," the midwife announced.

Lily was in and out of delirium as a frenzy of activity took place around her. Someone held a cloth to her mouth and she fell into a deep sleep with vivid dreams of her childhood, running through the fields towards her father.

Someone — she didn't know who — picked her up before she could run into her father's outstretched arms and carried her away, crying and screaming, "Daddy, no!" Then she was in her bed, in the cottage she shared with her parents. It was cold and she felt a chill. A shadow fell over her and when she opened her eyes, she saw Edmund Smith standing over her, grinning. As he moved towards her, she screamed.

When she finally awoke and recognised where she was, in her tiny bed in the cupboard behind the kitchen in the Williams residence where she worked as a scullery maid, Laura was sitting next to her, patting her face with a cool, wet cloth.

She tried to sit up, but Laura put a gentle hand on her shoulder and told her to lay down. Unable to fight the gesture, she said, "Where is my baby? Where is my son?"

But it was too late. Laura explained to Lily that he had already been removed from the townhome. The midwife would deliver him to a wet nurse and, after a week or two, once it was certain that he was healthy, he would be delivered to the countryside to be cared for until Lily was able to do so herself.

"No one told me I would not be able to see him. To hold him. To nurse him." She wept uncontrollably as Laura tried to comfort her.

"He had to be taken away at once," Laura told her. "If the family discovered that a baby had been born to one of the maids, out of wedlock, you would have been fired," she said. "It's for the best."

Mrs. Evans allowed Lily to stay in bed for three days before she told Laura to get her on her feet and back to work. Laura was only too happy to do so, since she had to manage the scullery maid duties while Lily was recovering.

The first day she managed to get out of bed and dressed, Lily visited Mrs. Evans in her office and asked for the location of her son.

The woman snorted a laugh, "You cannot see him while you are still in debt, Mary." She stood up and waved Lily out of her sight. "How would we be certain you would not kidnap him and disappear while you still owed money?

"I would never do that!" Lily protested.

"Then what use would it be to you to know the address of the kindly couple who agreed to take care of your child?"

"I should like to write a letter," she said. "To ask how he is doing. To ask what name they are calling him. To tell him that his mummy loves him and will come for him one day."

"A dreadful idea, and would only cause the child and his guardians distress," said Mrs. Evans. "Get back to work, and don't speak to me about this again until your debt is paid."

"But that could be years," Lily sobbed.

"You best get back to your duties lest I am required to dock your pay for this waste of time." Mrs. Evans turned her attention to her ledger and did not glance up again, indicating to Lily that she was dismissed.

Lily resumed her duties in a fog. She was often in pain but welcomed the physical pain to distract her from the ache in her heart. Although her son had been conceived in violence, he was *her* son and an innocent babe who she vowed to protect. She could not avoid feeling as though she had failed him.

She knew it would be years before she could pay off the debt to the nameless and faceless couple who were caring for her son. She prayed they were good, kind people and that the day would come when she would be reunited with the little boy that she had not even been given an opportunity to name. Each night before

she curled up on her tiny bed, she repeated the promise she made
that she would come to get him as soon as she could.

Although she missed the Coles, she was too ashamed to face
them after her decision to send her baby away. She was too
exhausted and depressed to even dream of spending a frivolous
afternoon being entertained by friends, so she sank into her own
dismal world of working and keeping a tally of her own ledger,
counting the weeks, months and years before she could pay off
her debt and be reunited with her son.

⚜

"MAY I HELP YOU?"

The downstairs door to the kitchen and servants' quarters had
been opened by a footman. While George Cole knew many of the
household servants from the neighbourhood since they
frequented the pub, he did not recognise this young man.

"My name is George Cole. I own the public house on Newton
Street, Holborn." He suddenly realised how odd his inquiry would
seem.

"Yes?"

George cleared his throat. "I'd like to inquire about your
scullery maid, Miss Lily Collins. She is a friend of the family and
was expected at supper yesterday, but did not arrive."

Gerald hesitated, looking George up and down. Then said,
"Wait here."

He shut the door, leaving George at the bottom of the
concrete stairs. A good ten minutes elapsed and George was
wondering whether the young footman had ever intended to
return. He leaned against the wrought iron bannister and gazed
up to the street level where passersby were going about their daily
business.

He finally heard a door open behind him and George turned
around, his attention returning to the reason for his visit. A

woman stood before him, a haughty look on her face, although her attire revealed that she was a household servant, most likely the head housekeeper.

"May I help you?" she asked. She kept her hand positioned on the doorknob as if to ensure she could quickly retreat inside if he became unruly.

Although George was certain that the footman had relayed his message and she knew exactly why he was there, he politely repeated himself. "Your scullery maid, Miss Lily Collins, is a friend of my family. I would like to see her for a moment. I promise I will not take more than a minute of her time."

He was guarded with his words. While he was certain this woman was likely aware of Lily's condition, he did not wish to reveal any more than was necessary, and certainly did not wish to reveal his relationship, or lack thereof, with the girl.

"Miss Collins is no longer employed at this house," she replied curtly. She pushed the door open again, just enough so that her slender frame could slip inside, and started to shut it in his face.

Stunned by her revelation, and seeing he had only a split second before the door closed, he blurted out, "Where did she go? When did she leave?" He desperately wanted to inquire about her health, her condition, and the health of the unborn baby, if indeed Lily was still pregnant.

"Even if I knew the answer to your questions, I would not be at liberty to reveal anything personal about any member of our staff, current or former. Good day." With that, the door shut firmly behind her.

❦

BREAKING THE NEWS TO ADA WAS NOT EASY. SHE HAD HER heart set on bringing a baby into their home, having realised years ago that she was unlikely to have a child of her own.

She wept when he told her what he had learned. He told her

he was sorry. He agreed with her that it seemed suspicious, that he was not convinced the housekeeper had told him the truth.

"What was I to do?" he asked. "I could not accuse her of lying with no evidence to the contrary."

Unfortunately, the servant from the Williams household who had been a regular at the pub, and had originally told George about the job opening to which he had steered Lily, had also disappeared. He would ask around among the regulars at the pub, but he did not want to call too much attention to his inquiries. Household servants were a closed knit group and, while they gossiped frequently among themselves, they were unlikely to give him information about a young maid who had come and gone from one of the households in a matter of months.

It was quiet in the Cole home for the next few months. Ada was morose, bordering on inconsolable.

As he trudged through his days at the pub with little to look forward to, George realised he was equally devastated, if not more so.

PART II

7

S *ix years later* ....

LILY STOOD UP FROM HER POSITION ON THE FLOOR AND stretched her back with a groan. That was the last fireplace on the main floor to clean out of ash. She was glad that her most physically taxing work was done in the morning. The rest of her day would be consumed with airing out the rooms, dusting the furniture, beating the carpets, and washing all the floors throughout the three-story townhome.

While the Williams family was eating breakfast, Lily tended to the bedrooms. Windows were opened, duvets shaken and aired, and chamber pots emptied. The water in the wash basin and pitcher was emptied and refreshed. Twice per week she would change the bed linens and wash the windows, inside and out. Brass fittings were shined, baseboards were wiped clean, picture frames dusted and woodwork polished.

In the years since giving birth, Lily kept her head down and fulfilled her tasks diligently. Mrs. Evans kept a close eye on her, but Lily would not give her any reason to be critical of her work. After she had been working as the household scullery maid for nearly two years, she was promoted to kitchen maid.

Mrs. Evans made it clear to Lily that her promotion was not a result of her good performance, rather because the cook's thirteen-year-old daughter was now ready to start working and would take over the position of scullery maid from Lily.

For the first two months, Lily was responsible for training Clara, who would now be called Mary, as well as learning her own new duties. It was difficult, but Mrs. Evans actually told her she would credit her account with an extra six-pence each week during her double duty. Anything that chipped away at her debt and brought her closer to seeing her son was fine in her mind.

Another year went by and Lily changed positions again, rising to become one of the minor housemaids. She did her job efficiently and with a pleasant countenance, which did not go unnoticed by Mrs. Williams, the lady of the house. Mrs. Williams appreciated servants who were neat and tidy and could be relied on to look presentable in front of guests.

When the chambermaid position became vacant — a result of old Mrs. Jones becoming far too feeble to handle the work — Mrs. Williams specifically requested that Lily be given the position, a request that Mrs. Evans was less than thrilled about, but could not refuse.

Every week, Mrs. Evans gathered the household servants in her office to hand over their pay envelopes. Lily received an envelope like everyone else, but instead of shillings and pence like the others, hers contained a single piece of paper with her week's wages noted, and the new balance of her debt at the bottom of the page. Lily watched expectantly as the amount was whittled away, week after week.

She was getting excited now, because it should only be another month before her debt would be paid and she would ask for permission to visit her son. It would be a little longer before she could hope to provide a home for him. She still needed to save money to find a room to rent so he could live with her, but she was confident that she could at least find a way to visit him until that time.

❦

IT WAS A SUNNY AUTUMN DAY, NOT THAT LILY NOTICED THE weather, so infrequently did she venture outdoors in the afternoon. Mrs. Evans had just handed out the pay envelopes to the servants, pausing longer than usual in front of Lily as she handed over the envelope with a deliberate nod of her head.

Lily raced up the back staircase to her room. She was living in the attic quarters now, having done so for the past few years since she had moved beyond the role of scullery maid. The small room was stifling in the summertime, but on this autumn day, a cool breeze came through the dormer window.

She ripped open the sealed envelope, hands shaking, and withdrew the single sheet of paper. On it was written in Mrs. Evans' unmistakably clear penmanship:

Miss Lily Collins
Statement of Wages
Balance forward -6 shillings
Earnings +7 shillings
Deductions -6 shillings
Payment due 1 shilling

INSIDE THE ENVELOPE, IN ADDITION TO THE STATEMENT OF account, was one shiny silver shilling.

Lily held the coin in her hand and gazed on it in amazement, like it was some foreign jewel that she had never before seen. She took a deep breath. She had done it. After six years, she was debt free. She could now save her wages, reunite with her son, perhaps even look for another job. She knew she was capable of so much more. She might even fulfil her father's dream of having her own handcart from which she would sell fresh fruit and vegetables in Covent Garden.

She recalled the first time she had accompanied Cook to Covent Garden to do the shopping. She could almost not contain her excitement. The sounds, the smells, the vendors, the children. She turned her head from side-to-side as she heard the shouts of merchants from her right, the cries of children from her left, the movement of handcarts barreling down the centre of the passageways.

That day, she had decided she belonged in this environment. She understood the fruit and vegetable market and she thrived with the buzz of Covent Garden. She also realised how much she missed being outdoors. And now she had paid off her debt, bringing her dream closer to reality.

There would be time enough for making plans. First she had a promise to fulfil. She descended the staircase to Mrs. Evans office, a lump in her throat as she had flashbacks to her previous encounters with the dreadful woman.

She took a deep breath as she stood outside of the office door and knocked, trying to appear more confident than she felt.

"Come in."

Lily opened the door and stepped into Mrs. Evans office, closing the door behind her. She knew that some of the other staff liked to hover around the open door and listen for any gossip that they could tuck away for later use.

"Mrs. Evans, may I have a word." Lily stood with erect posture, her hands clasped in front of her.

The older woman sighed in exasperation. "Not now, Miss Collins. Can you not see that I am busy?"

Truthfully, the woman did not appear busy at all. Her desk was tidy and when Lily had walked in she was locking away her ledger, a signal she had finished her paperwork for the day. Lily understood she would have to wait a little longer to obtain her son's location, but she would not be deterred by this ghastly woman.

She squared her shoulders and stood a little taller. "Then may I request an appointment that suits you for a brief conversation?"

The look of audacity on Mrs. Evans' face almost caused Lily to cower, but she stood her ground.

Finally, the woman consulted her diary, which looked empty from the distance Lily could see it, and said, "On Thursday at 2 o'clock. I can give you 10 minutes."

"Thank you," replied Lily, as she turned and left the office, closing the door behind her. She was tempted to slam it hard, but thought better of it. She would not offend the woman until she had what she wanted.

Thursday was still two days away but Lily had waited six years already. Another two days would not make much difference.

8

"Lily! Cook wants you to go to the market with her." Laura found Lily in the drawing room to give her the message.

Lily had grown quite fond of Laura over the years. Laura and Gerald were the only members of the household staff who had befriended Lily when she arrived. They both knew she'd given birth to a son and that he had been taken away, but neither of them had questioned Lily about the details.

Gerald initially seemed somewhat interested in developing a deeper relationship with Lily, but she pretended she did not understand his subtle hints and continued to treat him like a valued friend. She did encourage Laura to flirt with him, and after a while Gerald turned his attention to Laura. Lily was happy for them, but sad at the same time. She was lonely and craved companionship, even love, but she knew she needed to stay focused on finding her baby.

"Why aren't you going?" Lily asked Laura. As one of the primary kitchen maids, Laura was the logical choice to accompany Cook to Covent Garden to select the week's produce. Lily was secretly thrilled at the opportunity to go, however.

"There is extra work in the kitchen today. Mr. and Mrs. Williams are having dinner guests and there are an awful lot of vegetables to prepare. Plus, I know how you enjoy the market." Laura winked at her.

Lily also knew that whenever Cook was away, Gerald and Laura would find some time where they could sneak off and be alone. She returned Laura's wink with a smile, and gave her friend a brief hug before scurrying to the kitchen.

⚘

THE STREETS OF LONDON WERE CROWDED BUT LILY DID NOT mind. She was feeling positively ecstatic about her future. Yesterday she had cleared her debt and pocketed her first wage in six years and tomorrow she would get the address of her son's guardians. She would write a letter and they would soon be reunited.

What better way to spend today than a trip to Covent Garden. It almost seemed like fate that she should come here today of all days. This was the place she hoped to work someday and earn enough to make a home for herself and her little boy. It was a magical place with the vendors and costermongers shouting out their wares. Each stall was more enticing than the last and Lily had to take care to sidestep the many children, young girls selling flowers and colourful ribbons, boys dodging traffic with their barrows, racing through the narrow passageways.

"We'll have a bushel of new potatoes and a peck of onions. Maybe even some green beans if we can find them." Cook talked to Lily as she navigated the stalls. "If the strawberries are fresh, we'll buy enough for a cake to serve after tonight's dinner. Otherwise we'll settle on apples for a crumble. That reminds me, we could use some sugar as well. If it isn't too dear."

Lily went about assessing the ripeness of the fruit and looked for potatoes that weren't growing sprouts.

"Potatoes for you, madam!" shouted one of the stall vendors to Cook.

Cook approached the stall and squinted to assess the quality of the produce. Lily stood a little bit behind her.

"Best price at the market this week. You won't do better."

Cook nodded her head and the vendor reached for a bushel. Lily stepped forward and held up her hand to stop him. She reached down, picked up several potatoes and showed Cook the sprouts on the undersides. Cook scowled at the vendor and walked away.

A few feet away, a woman stood quietly behind her stand of fruit. Lily looked at her and she smiled. Lily approached the woman and asked, "When were the strawberries picked please?"

"About three days ago, miss. Best if they are used today or tomorrow."

Lily pointed to several pints which the woman picked up and handed to her. She turned over a few strawberries and pointed to those that had started to soften and brown.

"Five pints for the price of three," the woman offered. "That will make up for any that can't be used."

Lily nodded to Cook who accepted her suggestion and handed over the coins.

"Lily! Lily Collins! Is it really you?"

Lily was startled to hear her name called by a vaguely familiar female voice. She turned around from the direction of the cry and nearly crashed into a woman rushing to her. She did not immediately recognise the worn and rugged face, but just as she identified her, the woman spoke.

"It's Ada. Don't you recognise me?"

"Oh, Ada! Of course, I do. It was such a shock to see you here in front of me after all these years. I just need a moment to catch my breath."

The two women reached out to one another and hugged, then stood back, grasping hands, each assessing the other.

"Whatever happened to you, dear," Ada asked, her voice one of concern more than irritation that Lily had disappeared without a trace. "When you missed our regular supper, George went to your employer's residence to ask about you and they said you'd gone."

"They what? Who said that? I'm still at the Williams house. I never left." Lily had a flood of news she wanted to tell Ada, but now was not the time nor the place. "I'm so sorry I never sent word to you. I could not come that day because, well, that was the day that ...," she lowered her head, unable to finish the sentence.

"Miss Collins, we need to find the green beans," said Cook, tapping her foot impatiently.

"Can you come round? George and I would love to see you. Catch up on everything." Ada looked at Lily in earnest.

"I have the afternoon on Friday free. Around 2 o'clock? But don't go to any trouble. It will be just be good to see you both and catch up."

"Miss Collins!" Cook had found the coveted green beans and wanted Lily to judge their quality before she accepted them.

"Until Friday," Lily called over her shoulder to Ada as she dashed to catch up with Cook.

❦

LILY WRUNG HER HANDS AND SQUEEZED THE HANDKERCHIEF SHE held in them, aware that it was damp with her sweat. After six long years she was now on a path to a reunion with her son.

She sat quietly in the chair in front of Mrs. Evans desk. The housekeeper had gestured to her to sit down when she had arrived at her office two minutes before 2 o'clock on Thursday afternoon. Mrs. Evans returned her attention to her ledger and continued to write in it while Lily's anticipation grew.

Now it was nearly five minutes after 2 o'clock and Lily was

nervous because Mrs. Evans had only agreed to grant her ten minutes. Did these wasted minutes count?

Once she was satisfied that she had finished what she set out to do, Mrs. Evans snapped the ledger shut, laid down her pencil, and folded her hands on top of the book. She raised her head and finally gave Lily her full attention.

"Now, Miss Collins," she said. "You wished to speak to me."

"Yes, ma'am," Lily said. Her stomach clenched and she had to fight to keep her voice steady. She was aware that she needed to be swift and direct in her communication, so she decided to just blurt out her request. "I should like the contact information for my son. The address of his caretakers."

Mrs. Evans blinked, her face otherwise immovable. She said nothing for a moment, then furrowed her brow into a puzzled expression and said, "I don't understand."

Now it was Lily's turn to be puzzled. "My debt is fully paid. I should like to contact my son's caretakers. To write them a letter and find out how he is. Perhaps to visit him."

Surely this woman must have realised that she would be asking for this information as soon as her debt was paid. Mrs. Evans had told Lily years ago that she could revive her request for the information once that had happened.

"Why would you presume that I would have that information to give you?" Mrs. Evans was composed now.

Lily's eyes widened. "You arranged for his care. You found the couple that he was sent to live with until I could take care of him myself. You have been paying them half of my wages all these years." She knew she had to control her voice, which was becoming rather high-pitched in her alarm.

"I did no such thing." Mrs. Evans did not flinch, her voice remained even. She stared at Lily as if she had just made the most preposterous accusation.

"Excuse me?" Lily shifted to the edge of the chair and placed her hands on the desk in front of her. She squeezed the edge of the wood so hard she was certain she had permanently dented the polished oak.

"I contacted a woman who helped girls like you find a childless couple to adopt the baby you conceived out of wedlock. I then ensured he was delivered to her after you gave birth," said Mrs. Evans. "I advanced the 10 pound fee that she required to get you out of the trouble you had gotten yourself into. But all of that was over and done with years ago. I have no idea where your illegitimate son is now."

The blow of her final statement stung Lily as if she had been slapped in the face.

The colour had drained from Lily's face and she was light-headed. It was all she could do to keep herself from fainting as the woman's face became blurry in front of her eyes.

"No!" she said. She was crying now. "He was only to be cared for temporarily. I have been paying for his care all these years. With half of my wages. You've been paying it on my behalf. I must have the address of where he is living so I can find him." She was becoming desperate. Why was Mrs. Evans saying these things? Pretending that she did not know where her baby was.

"Miss Collins, compose yourself. I will not continue this conversation if you are going to be hysterical. I have told you that I do not know where your son was taken."

"Then where were half my wages going all these years? I was repaying the 10 pound fee plus the rest of my wages were going to pay for his care."

"What total nonsense. Wherever did you come up with a story like that? Your wages were garnished to pay for the crystal vase you broke when you were pregnant. Rather than tell Mrs. Williams that you knocked it over in your condition, I replaced it and you have been repaying it a little at a time."

"That's a lie! That never happened!"

"Of course it did." Mrs. Evans opened the ledger that was still on the desk in front of her. "You see, it is right here in the ledger. I replaced it with my own money because you were in dire straits. You've been paying it back all these years. Now your debt is paid."

Lily slipped from the chair with a thud as she fainted onto the floor of Mrs. Evans office.

9

The bony hand slapping her cheek was enough to bring Lily back to consciousness. She lifted herself to a sitting position on the floor, resting her arm on the seat of the chair out of which she had just fallen. Mrs. Evans walked to the office door and opened it, peering into the hallway to see if another servant was nearby to lend assistance.

"Gerald, fetch a glass of water," she said to the footman who happened to be on his way towards the panty.

When Gerald had delivered a glass of water, Mrs. Evans carried it to the desk, then grabbed Lily roughly under an arm and dragged her up. As she squeezed Lily's upper arm tightly, she handed her the glass of water and snapped sharply at her.

"Collect yourself and get back to work. This subject is closed if you want to continue your employment in this house."

Keeping her job was the last thing of concern to Lily at this point. The only thing that had kept her focused these past six years, through all the back-breaking work, was the promise she had made to her son. That she would reunite with him one day and they would have a future together.

She was weak from having fainted, and drained from the realisation that she had been deceived. She had been deceived for six years and robbed of her hard-earned wages.

She spoke quietly now. "Why are you lying? The money was to pay for my son's care until I could take care of him myself. You promised to tell me where he was."

Mrs. Evans spoke slowly, her voice cold and sinister, her pupils a black pinprick as she grabbed Lily's chin between her thumb and forefinger and squeezed hard.

"What do you plan to do about it, missy? Would you like to tell the mistress of the house? If you like, we can go together to Mrs. Williams and tell her about the child you bore out of wedlock, right here in her house shortly after we took pity on you and gave you a job. A job, I may remind you, you were completely unqualified for."

Lily dropped her head. The woman was right. She could no more admit to Mrs. Williams that she had given birth six years earlier than she could prove she had not broken a crystal vase for which she was paying for its replacement.

She stood up and walked slowly to the office door which had not been closed after Gerald had delivered the glass of water. This time when she exited, she slammed the door as hard as she had strength for, indifferent to any backlash from the woman on the other side.

As she slowly climbed the stairs to her attic room, she did not notice Gerald hovering in the corner behind the staircase.

LILY WAS DISCONSOLATE. SHE HAD NO IDEA WHERE TO TURN OR how to search for her son. She was certain she no longer had a job after her outburst with Mrs. Evans, but when she woke up the following morning and proceeded through her chores, no one treated her differently, the housekeeper was nowhere to be found, and she was not escorted to the door with her belongings as she'd seen done with previous staff who had been dismissed.

Today was the day she had promised to visit Ada and George and she was uncertain she could face them. Yesterday she had been so excited about the prospect of sharing her story with them. Telling them about the hardships of the past six years, but with news that her circumstances were about to change. She was going to find her son. Now all she had to tell them was how foolish she had been.

When she nearly bumped into Mrs. Evans on her way from sweeping the parlour, the woman gave her a look that nearly froze her in her path. Lily decided that taking the afternoon as far away from the house as possible would be a wise choice and good for her own mental health.

She collected her shawl, wrapped it tightly around her shoulders, slipped out of the lower level door, and dashed up the stairs to the street. The air was chilly and damp, but she savoured the freedom of the unconfined space. She was nearly a block away from the house and starting to relax when she heard someone calling her name and sensed heavy footsteps getting closer.

"Wait, Lily," Gerald shouted from behind. He was breathless when he reached her. "Didn't you hear me calling you?"

"Sorry, I guess I was in my own thoughts," she said.

"I want to give you something, but you can't say you got it from me." He pulled a crumpled piece of paper out of his jacket pocket and handed it to her. "That's the address where they took your baby."

Lily gasped. As she accepted the wadded paper, her heart skipped a beat. She opened it and tried to smooth the wrinkles to read the address.

Mildred Watson

44 Mervan Road
Brixton SW2

Lily held the note to her chest and squeezed her eyes shut tight until they watered. "How did you get this?"

"I was driving the carriage that day. The day he was born. The midwife gave me this paper with the address before they climbed into the carriage and I saved it all this time." Gerald looked down at the ground and kicked an imaginary stone with his scuffed boot. "I overheard what you said to Mrs. Evans yesterday. When I told Laura, and told her I knew where they took your baby, she said I had to tell you."

Lily's heart felt ready to burst and she threw her arms around Gerald's neck. He blushed and stumbled backwards, taken aback at her demonstrative gesture.

"I best get back to the house. They might be looking for me," he said, as he turned away.

"Thank you." Lily finally found her voice, although a simple thank you seemed hardly adequate. But Gerald has started running back to the townhouse so she did not have an opportunity to say more.

⚜

"I WILL GO THERE," GEORGE SAID TO LILY. "DON'T GET YOUR hopes up. It's been six years and it would be a miracle if the woman was still there and knew where your little boy was."

After Gerald had given Lily the address of where her son had been taken after she'd given birth, she contemplated going straight to Brixton. If she did not take advantage of her rare afternoon off, it would be weeks before she had another chance.

She recognised quickly, however, that it was impractical for her to make her way south of the Thames to Brixton in the short time she had. It would be dark before she could make her way back and she did not know the area. She would keep her promise to visit Ada and George and tell them everything. Perhaps they would have an idea of how to find her little boy.

Ada could almost not contain her shock as she listened to Lily's story, starting with the plan Mrs. Evans presented to turn her baby over to caretakers, to the day Lily went into labor and gave birth, the years of hard work to pay off her debt, Mrs. Evans subterfuge the previous day, and right up to the moment just hours earlier when Gerald gave her the address where her son was taken.

Ada's jaw dropped as Lily's story began and had not closed since, along with her gasps of "*oh, no*" and "*it cannot be so*" and "*you poor dear.*" She did not tell Lily of her original wish to adopt the child, but felt an ache in her own heart as she listened to the tale from this grief-stricken mother and thought about the newborn who had been separated from her at birth and could be almost anywhere now.

George listened quietly to Lily's entire discourse with anger rising as he considered the potential fate that had befallen the child. He read the newspapers and listened to the chatter in the pub about some of the tragedies that came to the working class and poor. He was aware of the baby farms and the unscrupulous women posing as nurses, swindling young women who were in trouble out of money with false promises that their children would be taken care of.

Lily also apologized to her friends for not having contacted them during the years. She bowed her head. "I was so ashamed that I had allowed my baby to be taken from me. That I could not provide a home for him. And I had no wages at all so I did not feel right about imposing on you for supper." A tear trickled down her check.

Ada reached out and patted her hand. "You have nothing to apologise for, dear. I wish we had tried harder to find you so we could have helped. Or at least been there to support you. You must have felt so alone and helpless."

That was when George spoke up and told Lily he would travel to Brixton to investigate. "You said he was supposed to be taken to a married couple in the countryside?"

"That's what I was told," Lily replied. "But everything else I was told turned out to be a lie. So I don't know if any of it is true." She sighed.

"I'll start with the address in Brixton. If we're lucky, someone will know something. Now let's have something to eat."

By the time they had eaten a light supper of bread and cheese together with some cider to drink, it was dusk. Lily looked out the window of the cozy rooms above the pub and said, "I better get back. I have an early day tomorrow and this week has been quite exhausting."

"I'll walk you home," George said. "It will be completely dark in a few minutes."

"I couldn't impose," said Lily. "You're doing so much for me already. I'm sure I'll be fine."

"No imposition at all." George was already pulling on his over-coat and scarf. "I could use the fresh air. Give me a chance to have a smoke on the way back."

Lily hugged Ada tightly as she said goodbye before she and George exited to the street. They walked slowly most of the way back to the Williams' residence. George told Lily about some of the regulars that came into the pub and even had her laughing at some of their antics. He told her he couldn't complain. He had a thriving business that earned a good income. Lily thought there was something wistful in the way he spoke of his life but she couldn't quite put her finger on it.

She wanted to ask him why he and Ada had no children but assumed there was a medical reason for it and did not want to embarrass him. They were both such kind and caring people that she thought it a shame they lived by themselves without the sounds of children playing and laughing.

"Here we are," George said, when they reached their destination. "Don't you fret now. If your son is out there somewhere, we'll find him."

10

George tugged at the collar of his overcoat to pull it closer around his neck in an attempt to protect himself from the chilly wind. The brick terrace houses on Mervan Road all looked identical and there was a heavy smell of coal burning in the air.

He thought seriously about how he would approach the occupant of the home when he arrived. From what he had read in the newspapers about some of the baby farming cases, he could not just barge in and demand to know where Lily's son was. He knew that this Mildred Watson, if indeed she was still engaged in such activity, would be cautious and evasive to a stranger asking questions, lest he be from the police.

He braced himself and knocked on the heavy wooden door. As he waited for any sign of life, he turned back to look at the street and nearby houses. It was eerily quiet with few people about, and those who were kept their heads down and avoided eye contact.

He heard a latch being opened behind him and turned his attention back to the door where a woman stood considering him. Her hair was a dull brown and pinned up on her head, her eyes sunken with dark circles beneath them. An apron was tied around her waist, over a worn dress made from heavy grey linen. George thought he heard a child's laughter in the background and his stomach clenched in anticipation of what he might discover.

"Yes?"

George tipped his hat and tried to smile to put the woman at ease. "Ma'am. I hope I'm not disturbing you, but it was recommended I seek help at this address."

The woman narrowed her eyes, but said nothing, waiting for George to explain himself.

He cleared his throat. "It's my sister. My younger sister. She is in a bit of trouble and I was told you might be able to help."

The woman's posture relaxed, her face softened. "I'm afraid I cannot help you. My husband and I have only lived here a year. The woman you seek is no longer here." She stepped back inside and started to close the door.

"Wait, please. Do you know where I might find her?"

The woman hesitated, considered him for a moment, and reopened the door. "You seem like a decent man. Take my advice, you do not want your sister to get the kind of help that was offered here. If she really is your sister."

George bowed his head. Should he tell her the truth? She may become angry if she knew he lied to her at the start. He had to chance it.

"Actually, ma'am, I am here on behalf of a friend. Her baby was delivered here six years ago and she is trying to find him."

The woman shook her head. "Tell her to give up. From what I hear, it was dreadful business. I don't know any of the details because we moved in long after the police cleared out the place. You might try asking down the station, or one of the neighbours. Old Mrs. Willet has been here forever. She's in number 38." She withdrew inside the house, shaking her head once again as she closed the door.

"Thank you, appreciate it, ma'am." His shoulders slumped and head lowered, George retreated down the path and found number 38.

⚜

GEORGE USED THE REST OF THE DAY TALKING TO OLD MRS. Willet and then prying what information he could from the chief constable at the Brixton police station. What they told him made his blood run cold and he had no idea how he would deliver the news to Lily.

As he feared, Mildred Watson was indeed involved in baby farming. She took money from young unwed women who had become pregnant in exchange for finding homes, some permanent and some temporary, for their children.

Some of the unfortunate women were prostitutes, some were mistresses of wealthy men who needed their illegitimate children to disappear. Some were innocent young women who had fallen in love and allowed themselves to be swept up in passion with a man who promised to marry them. And some, like Lily, were violated by their employers or men who held a position of authority over them.

Of even greater concern was that, in some cases, she found no homes at all for the babies.

"Gruesome business, that was," the chief constable told him. "One of the neighbours reported screams and what my men found when they went inside the place made grown men weep. There were five live babies, if you could call them that. They were in pitiable condition, underweight, hungry and filthy. The woman used laudanum to keep them drugged and quiet."

George felt nauseous as he listened, finding the information almost unbearable, and concerned about how, and exactly what, he would tell Lily.

According to the constable, evidence was found of multiple infant deaths. The five barely living infants were only a few of the hundreds that had been delivered to her care over several years. Mildred Watson was convicted of multiple counts of murder and hanged the previous year.

"Surprised you didn't hear of it," he said to George. "Was quite the story in the news at the time."

George had read about the case. He and Ada were sickened that there could be such monstrous people in the world. At the time, though, he had no reason to make a connection with Lily because he had no idea what had ever happened to her or her baby. Despite the horror of what he had learned, he found a glimmer of hope in something the constable said.

"She didn't start out that way. In the beginning, she really did try to find homes for the babies. But after a while, there were far more children than she could find couples to take them. She didn't want to give up the money she earned, so kept takin' 'em in and tried to care for them herself. After a while, she couldn't handle it. Couldn't feed them all or take care of them. That's when she started using the laudanum to keep them quiet. Claims she never meant to kill any of them. That they were casualties of an unfortunate situation. Yet she kept advertising in the locals and took in new ones all the time." The constable shifted in his chair and rubbed the back of his neck, a faraway pained expression on his face.

George sat up straight. "She found homes for them, you say? In the beginning? When would that have been?"

"Far as we can tell from the records we found, she started her operation about six or seven years ago."

"Records?" George asked. "Can I see the records you have from winter six years ago?" He was hopeful now. Perhaps he could go back to Lily with good news. He leaned in and held his breath.

The constable eyed him with suspicion. "I couldn't release confidential records, I'm afraid. That would be against policy."

George deflated, but had another idea. "What if the request came from an interested party? One of the mothers?"

"Not sure about that," the constable said. "I'd have to look into it. Won't say no, but can't say yes either."

11

Lily gripped her teacup tighter as she listened to George explain what he had discovered. She was overwhelmed with grief and Ada sat close to her, an arm over her shoulder, as she shook with tears listening to the fate of so many innocent babies.

George did not want to raise her hopes, but when he told her that there might be records of what happened to the earliest children placed with the woman, that many were indeed placed in legitimate homes around the time that Lily's son was taken, Lily's faith soared.

George leaned over and placed a reassuring hand on her arm. "It may not be possible to find him, Lily," he said. "Perhaps you can find some comfort in knowing that he was likely placed with a reputable couple. That he has thrived and grown. That he is happy now."

"I must try to find him," she said. "I promised him I would come for him. How would it be if his own mother never tried to find him."

"He has a mother, dear," said Ada. "I'm certain that the only mother he has ever known has looked after him as if she had given birth to him."

"No!" Lily cried, the tears flowing freely now. "If there is any chance he is out there, any chance there is a record of where he is, I must find him."

She stood up from the wooden table in the Coles' kitchen, nearly toppling the chair in her urgency, and wrapped her shawl around her. "I must go now. But thank you, George. I am so grateful for what you've done."

"Let me walk with you," he said. He glanced at Ada who studied him intently, then nodded as if to approve of his desire to accompany the distressed young woman.

LILY DID NOT REFUSE HIS OFFER AND SEEMED TO FIND COMFORT in his presence. Rather than walk directly back to her lodging at the Williams' townhouse, he steered her on a longer stroll through Russell Square. George thought it would have a calming effect on her.

They spoke of other things, more lighthearted in nature. He asked her about the trees, plants and flowers in the Square and she compared them to those in Hertfordshire, where she grew up with her parents.

George told her about his trips to purchase supplies for the pub and how he thought of someday expanding his business to wholesaling goods from the countryside to merchants in Covent Garden. Lily's eyes lit up as she spoke of her father's dream, that was now her dream. A dream for her and her son. George remembered that it was Lily who had first given him the idea, all those years ago when he first brought her to London.

"You must have put the idea in my head! I had no memory of where I'd thought of it." He laughed and she smiled.

Thinking of her dream brought her thoughts back to her baby.

"I am going to see the chief constable and ask him if I can see the records from when my son was taken." She said it quietly but deliberately, unwilling to be deterred. She looked straight ahead as they walked together side-by-side through the green gardens.

"Let me take you there," George said. "That way I'll know you're safe, and the constable knows me now. If he tries to deny you the information, I may be able to persuade him."

She stopped walking and turned to him. "Thank you, George. You're a good friend. I don't know what I would do without you and your wife."

"My wife?" George stared at Lily in bewilderment.

Lily observed his puzzled gaze, equally bewildered.

Suddenly George howled with laughter. "Ada?"

Lily nodded.

"Ada is my sister, not my wife," he almost could not control his laughter, so amusing was the idea to him that anyone could mistake his spinster sister for his wife. "I'm not married."

A myriad of feelings rose in Lily's chest. *Not married?* From the moment she had met George on the road to London, she felt an unspoken connection with him. At the time, she was still recovering from Edmund Smith's physical assault and then when they arrived in London, she immediately met Ada Cole. The woman she assumed was George's wife.

She had grown fond of them both in the succeeding months, when she would visit them for supper after she started working as a scullery maid, before she gave birth. Her heart would pound and her palms become sweaty when she saw George, and she sometimes caught him staring at her in a way that caused her some uneasiness. She could not quite comprehend what it was she felt for him, but between believing he was married and dealing with her own pregnancy and survival, as well as the excruciating workdays, she pushed any thoughts of him out of her mind.

George had stopped laughing. "Are you all right, Lily?"

She was aware that the color had drained from her face and she was feeling lightheaded. "Yes. Just feeling a little foolish. Silly me, making assumptions."

GEORGE SAID GOODBYE TO LILY AT THE KITCHEN DOOR ON John Street and told her he would collect her the following week when they would visit the chief constable together to ask for the records related to the time that Lily's baby was taken to Mervan Road.

He was aching to reach out and give her a hug, to kiss her cheek, but he held back and settled on a quick squeeze of her gloved hand. He felt a peculiar flutter in his belly, a feeling of pressure in his chest as he watched her retreat inside the town-house. She glanced back at him before closing the door, a slight curl of a smile on her lips.

George smiled back and raised a hand to wave but Lily had already closed the door. He turned and walked home, a million thoughts racing through his mind.

He had feelings for Lily the moment he laid eyes on her on the road to London. There was something so vulnerable about her, he felt the desire to protect her. He was uncertain whether his feelings went deeper, beyond a friendly concern for a fellow human being who appeared to need a guardian. By the time he decided to pursue a possible romantic relationship, Ada discovered Lily was pregnant.

Ada. His sister had suffered a tragic life of her own. As a young girl, she fell in love with a tailor's apprentice from Saville Row. They were inseparable and he told her they would be married as soon as he rose to a position of tailor. Once he became a tailor, he wanted his own shop.

Ada waited patiently over several years while Edward, her

fiancé, became more established. He had a growing list of clientele who asked for him when they came to the shop, but Edward was not satisfied. He wanted a shop of his own.

Ada begged him to start their life together. She told him she was proud of his accomplishments and they would have a fine life together, even if he remained working at one of the famous shops on Saville Row. But Edward was undeterred. He considered it a personal failure if he could not open his own establishment. An ambition he shared with several of his more affluent clients.

One of them, Lord Chesterton, offered to lend him the money to open his own tailor shop and Edward quickly accepted. He borrowed money to enter into a lease and more money to renovate the shop. When he could not pay his bills after several months, he borrowed more. Then disaster struck.

Lord Chesterton died and his heirs discovered the loans. Their own properties were in disrepair and in need of cash, so they called in the loans that Edward had taken. When he could not pay, he was sent to Debtor's prison.

Ada tried to visit him for months, but he refused to see her. He told her to move on and find someone else, but she was heartsick. She would wait for Edward for as long as it took him to get out of prison. Years passed before Ada learned that Edward had been released and disappeared.

By this time, George and Ada's parents had died and George had made a promise to them to look after his older sister. He inherited the pub from his father, made a success of the business and provided a stable home for himself and Ada. He had neither the time nor inclination to look for a wife of his own.

When Ada originally wanted to adopt Lily's baby, George thought it was a bad idea. She would be a single, unwed mother just as Lily would be if she kept the child. But Ada pleaded with him.

"I shall never marry now, and even if I did, I am past my childbearing years. Please, George. I need to do this."

George had his own feelings for Lily by this time. Although they would be an unconventional family, he planned to ask Lily to marry him. He would become a father to her child and Ada would be the child's nanny, if Lily did not object. He was convinced they could be a happy family and could raise the child in a loving home.

Then Lily disappeared without a trace. He berated himself for not trying harder to find her after he'd been told she had left her employment at the Williams' residence. He should have suspected something was not right.

If it was the last thing he did, he would make it up to her and to Ada. He would help Lily find her son.

12

It was their third visit to the Brixton police station and the second time they would meet the chief constable. Their first visit yielded no result at all. The chief constable with whom George had originally spoken was not at the station that day, and no matter how hard he tried to get one of the lesser officers to speak to him, they insisted he and Lily would have to return when the senior officer was available.

Weeks after the first unsuccessful visit, they tried again, having previously confirmed the best day and time to meet the chief constable. Scheduling the visit on the same day as Lily's free afternoon proved to be challenging, but they managed.

Lily breathed a sigh of relief when they were ushered into the chief constable's office. But her relief would be short-lived.

"I'm sorry you came all the way out here, Miss Collins," he began. "As I told Mr. Cole previously, we are unable to release any confidential records from any criminal cases, either opened or closed. It could compromise justice."

"But the woman was convicted and hanged. Justice has already been served. My son may still be alive and living nearby.

Reviewing the records from the time he was taken might lead to his rescue."

"Miss Collins, if he was adopted, there is nothing to rescue him from. I'm sorry to tell you that either the boy is living a good life or he is dead. Either way, I cannot help you."

Lily was aghast at his callousness and her agitation was palpable. George had to calm her and intervene with the constable. By the time they left the station that day, George had persuaded the man to retrieve the records, at least for the month before and after Lily gave birth. They would tackle an expanded record search if it produced no result. The records were held at another location, so the chief constable again had to ask George and Lily to return before he could turn over the requested documents.

Lily was shaking as they exited the station, George trying his best to calm her.

"We must remain calm but resolute," he said. "A man like that cannot be pushed, and the more upset one becomes with him, the less cooperative he will be."

"When he said my son could be dead, so flippantly, as if he was suggesting that he could either be in Sussex or Devon, I wanted to scream."

"I know, dearest, and I'm sorry you had to go through this ordeal," he said, as they walked away, arm in arm. "But we succeeded in persuading him to retrieve the files and will return in a fortnight. Hopefully, we will be closer to finding your little boy at that time."

George and Lily had become closer since they began their quest together to find Lily's child. Once she discovered he was a bachelor, and he understood that her earlier reticence was not indifference, they fell naturally into a comfortable rhythm, an unspoken feeling between them that once they had exhausted the mystery of Lily's baby, they would pursue their relationship.

They arrived back at the Cole residence above the pub and briefed Ada on the outcome of their visit. Ada was tickled George and Lily were becoming closer, and had chortled heartily when George told her that Lily thought Ada was his wife.

After supper, George walked Lily home before returning to help Ada with the washing up.

"What are the chances of finding him?" Ada asked her brother. "It will devastate her if she does not find him, or at least find out what happened to him."

"I know," George said. "We will have to deal with that when the time comes. She is a young woman and, if she will have me, I will give her many more children."

❧❦❧

LILY'S WORKING DAYS WERE STILL LONG AND PHYSICALLY demanding. The time in between her free afternoons dragged interminably. Those were the days she could see George, with whom she was becoming very fond. And, of course, those were also the days they could continue their search.

Gerald often asked her if she had been able to discover anything from the address he gave her. While she was grateful for what he'd done, Lily was guarded about revealing the status of her inquiries. First, she knew she may never find the answer. The fewer people who were privy to the details, the easier it would be to put the outcome behind her, whether successful or not. Second, Lily knew that Gerald would likely tell Laura whatever she told him, and before long, the other servants would know. Which would get back to Mrs. Evans. And Lily certainly did not want Mrs. Evans to know she was investigating the whereabouts of her son.

George came by whenever possible to see Lily, even if only for five minutes. She was permitted a lunch break and sometimes she would spend her time with George rather than eating in the kitchen with the other servants.

Finally, she had another mid-week afternoon off when George

had agreed to take her to Brixton station to hear if the records had been made available for them to review.

For the third time, George and Lily sat in the grey metal straight-backed chairs across from the chief constable's desk. He folded his hands on his desk blotter and, for the first time in all their visits, appeared genuinely somber.

"I'm afraid I have bad news," he began.

Lily grasped George's upper arm and could not avoid squeezing it hard. Was the constable going to tell her that he had found evidence that her son had perished? The colour drained from her face as she waited for him to continue, and George held her hand.

"The records from the Mervan Road case were archived after the trial ended and Mildred Watson was hanged. Unfortunately, it appears they were archived at the station in Southwark, shortly before the great fire at Cotton Wharf. I'm sorry to tell you that the records were destroyed."

Lily slumped over and would have slipped from her chair had George not caught her.

"Are you absolutely sure?" George asked. "Is there any possibility whatsoever that the records we are looking for were not in that fire?"

Lily started to cry softly.

"My clerk tells me that all of the documents that were presented at trial were archived," said the constable.

George had an idea. "What if the records from Miss Collins' son were not presented at trial. For example, if he was indeed placed in a foster home, or was adopted legitimately?"

The chief constable sprang to his feet. He was becoming almost as dedicated to solving the case as George and Lily, having grown a soft spot for the couple.

"If they were not part of the trial record, we should still have them in the basement files right here," he exclaimed. "*Roberts!*" He shouted for his clerk.

It was over an hour before the clerk returned to the chief's office, time that dragged endlessly to Lily. For lack of anything better to discuss, George and the constable talked about the sport of angling, and later debated the downfall of drink. George, being a pub owner, and the constable, the observer of far too many alcohol-related mishaps, were able to have a lively discussion despite their obvious differences.

Finally, the clerk knocked on the door and carried a thick file into the office.

"These are the files of children who were passed directly along from Mervan Road to foster families in the countryside, sir," he explained. "Many of them spent no more than a few days at Mervan Road before they were placed in alternate care locations. This is the list from the period you requested."

He handed over a ledger of several pages with dates, names, fees and addresses on it. The constable spread the large sheets on his desk and the four of them — George, Lily, the constable and the clerk — leaned over them and started to read.

"Here is something," George said, reading aloud. But as he did, he figured the details did not match.

When all four of them had scrutinised the first page and nodded they were finished, the clerk turned the ledger to the next page. They searched the document for about twenty minutes and had made it to page 3 of the ledger covering the days around the birth of Lily's son.

The constable nudged George discreetly and pointed to an entry.

"What about this one?" he said under his breath. He did not want Lily to hear, lest she get her hopes up.

George scanned the entry.

- *November 23rd*
- *Newborn boy*
- *mother — scullery maid*
- *father — unknown*
- *custodian — M. Evans*
- *paid £10*
- *John Street, Bloomsbury*

"Lily, look at this one. This has to be him." George said excitedly.

The entry continued with the name and address of a couple in Watford.

"Mr. and Mrs. Simon Ward, Granville Road, Watford," Lily read aloud from the page. She whispered a silent prayer, "Please, God, let him be safe, healthy and happy. I'm coming for you, darling."

13

"I should like to ask for two days free." Lily stood in front of Mrs. Evans desk for the first time since the woman refused to tell her the whereabouts of her son. She had little choice. It would be impossible to travel all the way to Watford and back on one of her free afternoons.

"May I ask what would be the reason for your request to neglect your responsibilities for two full days, Miss Collins." Mrs. Evans pursed her lips together in a tight line and wrinkled her nose as if a foul stench had invaded the room.

"It's a personal matter, ma'am," Lily answered.

"Would it have anything to do with the man that visits you when you should be tending to your chores?"

Lily took a deep breath and attempted to remain stoic. Both she and Mrs. Evans knew that George never interrupted her work and only visited when Lily had a lunch break, and rarely for more than a few minutes. It would be ill-advised to argue with her, however, so Lily did not try to contradict her. She knew it was an attempt by the woman to bait her into an argument so she could refuse her request.

"Indirectly, ma'am," Lily said. "Mr. Cole believes he may have found my son and I should like to visit him."

Mrs. Evans sprang up from her chair, her face twisted in rage, veins popping in her scrawny neck. "Absolutely not!" she screamed. Her nostrils flared like a horse with distemper. "I forbid it. If indeed it is the child you bore, he has a new life and home now. Nothing good can come of you seeking him out. Get back to work at once."

Lily turned and ran from the room, the echo of the woman's voice pounding in her ears. She ran up the stairs, pulse racing and heart pounding, gritting her teeth hard to keep from shouting out in frustration. She could not face the other servants, most of whom were in the kitchen. The parlour was likely empty at this time of day so she would seek some solitude there. She would feign checking on the fire although it was certain to not require tending for another hour or two.

As she raced into the parlour, unable to hold back the tears that blurred her vision, Lily collided with the lady of the house, Mrs. Williams, knocking them both to the floor with a loud thud.

"Oh!"

"My word!"

Lily wiped her eyes and discovered whom she had just knocked off her feet. "I am so sorry, Madam! Please forgive me. I ... I did not know anyone was here." Lily swallowed hard and tried to spring to her feet to help Mrs. Williams up, despite being off balance herself.

"My heavens, Lily," the mistress of the house said. "Why are you in such a hurry? You must be more careful."

The embarrassing incident combined with her argument with Mrs. Evans was too much for Lily. She was overcome with emotion and could hold the tears back no longer. She burst into tears and wept openly.

Mrs. Williams became flustered by the girl's reaction. "Never mind dear, there was no harm done. There is no need to cry."

The kindness from her mistress caused Lily to become even more overwhelmed. She crumpled to the floor, drew her legs to her chest, and wept.

※

ONCE MRS. WILLIAMS HAD MANAGED TO CALM LILY AND reassure her that she was in no trouble from the collision, the lady of the house withstood convention and insisted the distraught housemaid sit beside her on the sofa and tell her what was wrong.

By this point, Lily felt she had nothing to lose and poured her soul out to the woman. She assumed she was likely to be dismissed by the end of the day anyway, whether by Mrs. Williams or Mrs. Evans. Perhaps it was for the best. She could use the time to find her son and then worry about getting another job later. In the months since she had paid off her debt, she had managed to save most of her wages while George and she used the necessary time to uncover information about her son from the Brixton chief constable.

The last thing Lily anticipated was her mistresses reaction to her story.

"You must take the days you need at once," she said. "You poor dear. All these years you were unable to see your baby. I wish you had confided in me from the start."

"But Mrs. Evans forbid me from taking the days off," Lily said.

"You leave that to me. When did you wish to travel to Watford? Do you have transport?"

Lily's head was whirling with thoughts. "The day after tomorrow. Mr. Cole said he would arrange transport." *Was this really happening? Was she obtaining permission to go find her son from the lady of the house?*

The last thing Lily expected was the silver coin that Mrs. Williams pressed into her palm.

"Shh, it will be our secret," she said. "Good luck, Miss Collins. Go with God."

⁂

THE ROADS WERE BUMPY AND RUTTED FOLLOWING THE RECENT rains and the carriage ride quite uncomfortable, but to Lily, she felt like a queen on a grand adventure. It was certainly a more luxurious journey than her original trip to London, now more than seven years earlier.

Lily had risen early, before the sun, and with Mrs. Williams' blessing and encouragement had packed some day-old bread and cheese for the journey. She donned her worn coat, the ragged shawl wrapped around her neck, and stepped outside, clutching the meagre refreshments in one hand, the address of her son's caretakers in the other, while she waited for George to arrive.

The sun came up to warm them before they reached the outskirts of London and Lily's eyes remained glued to the carriage window. She was excited to see green fields again, it being years since her world consisted of nothing more than a few square miles of the City.

After a few hours, George told her they were at the Watford city limits. Lily's stomach started to churn and she feared she would be sick. At the north end of Granville Road they alighted from the carriage. They did not have the exact address of Mr. and Mrs. Simon Ward's home, but would knock on doors from one end to the other until they found the couple that had adopted Lily's son.

"I guess we just start knocking and asking," George said. He looked at the young woman he had grown to adore over the past several months and his heart ached for the strain he could see she was under. "Are you ready?"

Lily nodded and for the next hour they had doors closed in their faces, doors that were never opened although they could see occupants behind curtains, and doors opened by sympathetic souls who would said they would like to help but had never heard of the Wards.

At the south end of the road, after they had knocked on all the doors on one side without luck, they reached The Crescent where they sat on a bench and ate the bread and cheese that Lily had brought from London before tackling the opposite side. At the second house, their luck changed.

"I knew Mr. and Mrs. Ward. Nice couple," said the elderly man who had answered the door.

"Can you tell us which number is their house?" George asked while Lily held her breath.

"Number 28 they had. Or was it 26? It was one of those. But you won't find 'em there."

This time Lily spoke up, unable to contain herself. "Did they move? Do you know where? Would you have their address please, sir?"

"They didn't move. The typhoid got 'em. It was quite the epidemic in these parts last year. Or has it been two years already?"

"They died?" George asked, deflated. "Do you remember they had a child? A little boy? Do you know what happened to him?"

"They had a couple of children," he said. "Pretty sure a girl and a boy. One of 'em died too, along with the parents. The boy I think."

George instinctively reached out to steady Lily, knowing without looking at her that she was likely to go weak at the knees.

"Or was it three youngsters?" The man removed his spectacles and started to polish them on his shirttail. "Let me ask my wife, she would remember."

He shuffled into the house, leaving George and Lily standing at the doorway for several minutes before returning.

"My Martha tells me it was three young children. Two boys

and a girl. One of the boys died the same time as the parents. He was not even walking yet, just a toddler."

"You said this was a year or two ago?" George asked.

"Yes, sir. Remember it clearly because Martha could still get around pretty well and would take soup to the afflicted. Not long after, she lost the use of her legs."

"It could not have been him," Lily said to George, clearly becoming excited. "If it was two years ago and the boy was a toddler, it isn't him. He would have been older than that." She turned to the elderly man and said, "Do you know what happened to the other two children, sir? The other boy and the girl?"

"I asked Martha that very question. She was quite certain they were taken to the London Orphan Asylum over near Watford Junction. It's not far from here."

14

George could almost not keep up with Lily as she raced in the direction of Watford Junction at an accelerated pace. They were both breathless by the time they reached the large complex of brick buildings that housed the London Orphan Asylum. From the entrance near the railway they saw the chapel. A bit of a distance away was what appeared to be the administration building.

They had managed to explain the purpose of their business to the head mistress, Mrs. Edwards, who was somewhat taken aback that they did not know the Christian name of the child about whom they were seeking information. George tried to explain the entire story in as concise a manner as possible to the woman.

George and Lily were asked to take seats in the reception area while Mrs. Edwards attempted to find what, or rather who, they were looking forward. After nearly forty-five minutes, a severe looking secretary with her hair in a tight bun ask them to return to Mrs. Edwards' office.

They sat down in wooden chairs in front of Mrs. Edwards' desk and clutched hands in anticipation. Their journey had brought them this far and if their visit today did not reap any reward, Lily did not know where she would turn from here.

"Henry and Eliza Ward are indeed in residence her at the asylum," Mrs. Edwards said.

Lily's heart was pounding so hard she was certain it could be heard. "Henry? His name is Henry." She choked on the words. "Is he healthy? Is he happy?"

Mrs. Edwards smiled. "He is well. Henry is now 7 and his sister, Eliza, is 4 years old. They have been living here since the tragic passing of their parents nearly two years ago."

Lily swallowed hard at the mention of the Wards as her son's parents. "Can I see him now? Can he go home with me?"

"Oh, my goodness, no, Miss Collins. That would be terribly confusing and disrupting to the child."

"But I'm his mother. Can I see him at least, until I can arrange for him to return to London to live with me?"

"We could arrange for you to visit briefly with him, but it would be impossible for you to take him away from here," Mrs. Edwards said. "As far as I understand, you are still not married, is that right?"

"Yes, but ...,"

"We look after the children here until we are able to find a proper home for them. With both a mother and a father."

George had been watching the exchange quietly for several minutes, but before Lily had another chance to object to Mrs. Edwards decision, he spoke up.

"Perhaps we did not properly introduce ourselves. Miss Collins and I are engaged to be married," he said. "I am her fiancé." He looked quickly at Lily in an attempt to signal to her to not appear surprised by his statement. He squeezed her hand.

"I see," said Mrs. Edwards. "Once you have married, we would certainly review your application to adopt a child from our institution. There is a slight problem with that child being Henry, however."

Lily's stomach clenched. There was something wrong with her son? Her darling little boy, after it had taken her all these years to find him?

George asked, "And what is that?"

"He has a sister, Eliza. The children are very close, devoted to one another. We would never agree to split them."

Lily released the breath she'd been holding and started to laugh, as did George. She looked at the man who had just become her fiancé seconds earlier, and the two of them nodded at one another.

"Of course, we would adopt Eliza as well," George said. "We would not dream of splitting up the children."

There was a knock on the door and Mrs. Edwards' secretary opened it cautiously, with a nod to the mistress.

"I must caution you," Mrs. Edwards said to Lily, looking her in the eye with a stern gaze. "It would be extremely disorienting to the child to tell him you are his mother the first time you meet him. If you agree you will refrain from doing so, you may see him now. In time, he will learn you are his mother."

Lily clasped her hands against her belly, the butterflies were so intense she felt she needed to calm them. "I understand," she said, trying her best to appear calm and composed to prove she was ready to see Henry.

Mrs. Edwards nodded to her secretary and the door was opened wider, allowing a young boy with naturally curly brown hair and wide eyes to enter.

Lily's heart skipped a beat and George held her hand tightly.

"Henry," said Mrs. Edwards. "This is Mr. and Mrs. Cole." She used the surname George had given her as if the pair were already married. "They would like to meet you."

Lily leaned down in order to be eye level with her son. Henry approached her tentatively and looked into her face.

"Hello, Henry," she said.

"Hello, Miss," said the boy as he reached up a hand to her face and touched her cheek. "Why are you crying? Are you sad?"

"No, darling." Lily sniffed as she took Henry's hand and pressed it against her cheek. "Those are happy tears."

EPILOGUE

Three years later ...

Covent Garden Market was a bustle of activity, teeming with merchants and patrons alike. It was nearly impossible to move through the crowds as children darted between the legs of the adults and the costermongers shouted for attention, each trying to outdo the other.

"Two a penny!"

"Bushel for a six-pence!"

"My boy will bring it round for you, madam!"

"The best beans, just in from France!"

The cacophony was deafening but Lily loved every minute of it. She and the children spent most of Tuesday and Saturday mornings selling the ripe fruits and vegetables that she and George had sourced from the countryside on their frequent trips to collect supplies for the pub. He had told her they could live just fine on the income the public house brought in, but she wanted to fulfil her father's dream, and her own dream, of selling in the market, at least for a while.

She had not told him yet, but she had a suspicion that she was with child and would be giving up the handcart shortly. Once she had the new baby, she would stay closer to him and help in the pub, perhaps preparing the daily ploughman's, meat pies and boiled eggs.

They still lived above the pub, in the rooms where Lily first visited George and Ada. The occupants of the adjacent rooms had moved out two years earlier which allowed them to expand their space and keep Ada nearby. She had tried to find other accommodation and let the young, instant family have their privacy, but Lily would hear nothing of it.

"You should have your own private space without an old spinster getting in your way at every turn," Ada said.

"Nonsense," said Lily. "Besides, whatever would the children and I do without you."

Henry and Eliza adored Ada and she them. When George and Lily first got married and brought the children home, only a week after their visit to the orphan asylum, Ada was a godsend. The children were reticent and frightened by their new surroundings and new parents and Ada seemed to have a soothing and calming effect on them that neither George nor Lily quite managed at the start.

Lily was also working at the Williams residence for a full month after getting married, until they were able to find a suitable replacement for her. Several of the other servants scoffed and told her she should just leave immediately and let Mrs. Evans deal with her absence. But Lily felt she owed it to Mrs. Williams to ensure an easy transition, after the mistress had been so kind to her and particularly since Lily's duties were mainly carried out in the main part of the house that her employer enjoyed.

Once Lily quit her job, Ada said she would find her own accommodation but seemed happy, not to mention relieved, when the extra space became available and George and Lily insisted they rent the additional rooms so she could remain with their expanding family.

Even now, Ada tended to the children whenever George and

Lily traveled to pick up supplies for the pub and fresh fruits for the market. Occasionally, Henry would accompany his parents on their journey to the countryside, but Eliza seemed to prefer staying back and spending time with Ada.

"Fresh strawberries!" Henry called out to the passersby at the marketplace. "Six-pence for a peck."

"I'll take a peck," said a young woman.

Henry scrambled to serve the woman, selecting a peck of the plumpest and finest strawberries as Lily had taught him. The woman handed him a shilling and said to him, "I have something coming back from that coin, young man."

"Yes, ma'am, six-pence change." He turned to Lily who had been serving another customer at the opposite side of the handcart.

When Lily turned around to give her attention to Henry as he completed the sale of strawberries, the two women exclaimed simultaneously.

"Laura!"

"Lily!"

"And Gerald, too," said Lily, as she rushed around the handcart to embrace her friends.

Laura and Gerald were shopping for the Williams residence, this time without Cook, who now trusted her long-serving staff to select the freshest items at the best price.

As Lily hugged Laura, she felt the protruding belly on the girl, looked down, then back up into Laura's glowing face and smiled.

"We got married," said Laura quickly. "Three months ago."

"I'm so happy for you both," Lily said, squeezing the two of them again in a bear hug.

"Your six-pence, miss," said Henry, staring up at his mother and the two strangers she was embracing.

The three adults laughed and Laura leaned over to accept the silver coin from Lily's son.

"Thank you, young man. What is your name?"

"I'm Henry. This is my sister, Eliza," he said pointing to his sister who was hiding behind her mother's skirts. "And this is my mummy." He reached up and took Lily's hand, as if she might slip away from him if he didn't hold on.

"It's very nice to meet you, Henry. I'm Laura and I'm an old friend of your mummy. We haven't seen each other in some time, and I'm happy to see you are taking such good care of her."

Henry beamed and even Eliza peeked out from behind Lily to get a better look at her mummy's friend.

※

"I saw Laura and Gerald at the market today," Lily told George and Ada over supper. "They were recently married and Laura is expecting a baby."

"How wonderful," Ada said. "A newborn baby is such a blessing in a home."

"That it is," said Lily. She gazed over at her husband with an adoring look that told him she felt like the luckiest girl in the world.

THE END

ABOUT THE AUTHOR

Tillie Walker is an emerging author of historical Victorian romance and family sagas.

Tillie grew up in Tring, Hertfordshire, UK and lived in London for a decade before retreating back to the English countryside. She studied history and literature at university and used her knowledge as a volunteer tour guide at some of London's most visited landmarks.

Strolling the famous streets of London led to her interest in writing historical fiction set in the Victorian period.

"My favorite author growing up was Charles Dickens which was a primary reason for choosing my majors at university. I hope my stories will give readers a vivid sense of what it was like in the late 19th century in England."

Printed in Great Britain
by Amazon